DUNJA JOGAN

FELIX AFTER THE RAIN

Translated by Olivia Hellewell

#FelixAftertheRain

For teacher resources and more information,
visit www.tinyowl.co.uk.

Original title: Srečkov kovček
Author: Dunja Jogan
First published by Založba Zala / Zala publishing, Slovenia, 2017.
Published in the English language by arrangement with Zala Publishing, Hlebce, Slovenia.
First published in the UK and the US in 2020 by Tiny Owl Publishing, London.

A catalogue record for this book is available from the British Library.
A CIP record for this book is available from the Library of Congress.

UK ISBN 978-1-910328-45-3
US ISBN 978-1-910328-58-3
Printed in China

This book has been selected to receive financial assistance from English PEN's PEN
Translates programme, supported by Arts Council England. English PEN exists to promote
literature and our understanding of it to uphold writers' freedoms around the world, to
campaign against the persecution and imprisonment of writers for stating their views,
and to promote the friendly co-operation of writers and the free exchange of ideas.
www.englishpen.org

DUNJA JOGAN

FELIX AFTER THE RAIN

TINY OWL

Felix was a terribly unhappy boy.

He dragged an enormous suitcase behind him wherever he went.

But he didn't know what was inside.

Something dark had appeared in the suitcase
when Grandma died.

Something hurtful had hidden inside
when his friends made fun of him.

Something bothersome had burrowed its way in
when his Dad told him off.

The suitcase became heavier and heavier.

Felix could barely manage to push it along.

If only he could leave it somewhere
and escape across the ocean.

But the sea was so rough
and the winds were so wild.

Grandma used to say to Felix
that the sun always shines after the rain
and that after every uphill climb
there's a downhill stroll.

One day, Felix reached the top of the hill, puffing and panting.
He lay down in the shade and fell asleep.

A small boy was playing nearby.
He caught sight of the suitcase, crept toward it and opened it up.

All of a sudden,
the sky turned gray.

Felix found himself
in the middle of a storm.

He felt a rumble in his head, and his eyes filled
with tears that ran down
his cheeks like the rain.

When the storm had settled,
Felix felt calm too.

“What did you do with
the suitcase?”
he asked the curious boy.

He just smiled,
and Felix thanked him.

Felix came down from the hilltop
and he looked at
the clouds in the sky.

He smelled the blossom on the trees and
listened to the hum of the friendly breeze.

Without a care in the world,
he leapt towards the clear blue sea.

"I feel like a fish in water!"

He returned home empty handed
but with a heart full of happiness.

It lifted him off the ground like a balloon.

Felix was so happy,
he wanted to give
everyone a hug.

And everyone gently
hugged Felix.